Rabbids Invasion

Case File #4: Rabbids Go Viral

by David Lewman

illustrated by Patrick Spaziante

Simon Spotlight

New York London Toronto Sydney New Delhi

This book is a work of fiction. Any references to historical events, real people, or real places are used fictitiously. Other names, characters, places, and events are products of the author's imagination, and any resemblance to actual events or places or persons, living or dead, is entirely coincidental.

Based on the TV series Rabbids® Invasion as seen on Nickelodeon™

SIMON SPOTLIGHT
An imprint of Simon & Schuster Children's Publishing Division
1230 Avenue of the Americas, New York, New York 10020
This Simon Spotlight paperback edition February 2015
© 2015 Ubisoft Entertainment. All rights reserved. Rabbids, Ubisoft, and the Ubisoft logo are trademarks of Ubisoft Entertainment in the U.S. and/or other countries. All rights reserved, including the right of reproduction in whole or in part in any form. SIMON SPOTLIGHT and colophon are registered trademarks of Simon & Schuster, Inc. For information about special discounts for bulk purchases, please contact Simon & Schuster Special Sales at 1-866-506-1949 or business@simonandschuster.com.
Manufactured in the United States of America 0115 OFF
10 9 8 7 6 5 4 3 2 1
ISBN 978-1-4814-2766-1 (hc)
ISBN 978-1-4814-2765-4 (pbk)
ISBN 978-1-4814-2767-8 (eBook)

CHAPTER 1:
Whack-a-Rabbid!

One sunny day a bunch of kids were enjoying a fun birthday party in a city park. The park was very nice, with lots of green trees and bushes.

The kids were having a great time running around, laughing, and looking forward to eating so much ice cream their stomachs would ache.

Little did they know they were being watched.

Underneath one of the biggest, bushiest bushes were three Rabbids, those mysterious invaders from who knows where! They were lying on their pudgy stomachs, watching the happy kids, fascinated.

"Bwoooooh," one of them said, staring at the kids running and skipping.

"Bwah!" said another Rabbid, pointing. The other two Rabbids quickly turned their heads in the direction he was pointing.

An adult hung a colorful piñata shaped like a pig from a tree branch. "Okay, kids!" yelled another adult. "Piñata time!"

The kids cheered and ran over to the tree. A woman carefully tied a bandana around the eyes of the birthday boy.

The Rabbids' eyes got big. What in the world was going on?!

A man handed the boy a baseball bat. Then he gently spun the boy around in a circle. When he was done, he let the boy go and said, "Good luck!"

Feeling a little dizzy, the boy wobbled a bit. Then he started poking around the air with the bat. Finally, he touched something. *Tap! Tap!* The piñata!

He pulled the bat back and swung it around as fast as he could. *WHACK!* The piñata swung on its rope. The boy kept swinging his bat. *WHACK! WHACK! WHACK!*

Underneath the bush the Rabbids looked at each other, puzzled. What had that pink creature done to deserve all this whacking?

The pig piñata started to crack. The boy gave his bat a tremendous swing and . . . *CRACK!* The piñata broke open and candy spilled out!

"Bwaaaah," the Rabbids said, amazed by what they were seeing.

The other kids squealed and laughed, diving for the candy and grabbing at it.

The Rabbids crawled out from under their bush and ran toward the candy. But by the time they got there, the kids had scooped up all the candy and left to go eat so much ice cream their stomachs would ache.

The three Rabbids hung their heads, disappointed that the candy was gone.

But one of the Rabbids stared at one of his fellow Rabbids. In his mind, the other Rabbid turned into a colorful pig. A pig full of candy. This gave the first Rabbid a brilliant idea!

He grabbed the left ear of the other Rabbid. "Bwah! Bwah! Bwah! Bwah!" he yelled to the third Rabbid, motioning for him to grab the other ear.

"BWAAAAH!" shouted the Rabbid whose ears were being grabbed.

The two Rabbids hoisted the third Rabbid up in the air and tied his ears to the branch of a tree. Then the first Rabbid put on a blindfold, then picked up a handy toilet plunger and waggled it. Sticking his tongue out in concentration, he got ready to whack candy out of his fellow Rabbid!

When the tied-up Rabbid realized what was

about to happen, he yelled, "BWAAAH! BWAAAH! BWAAAH!" The Rabbid on the ground swung his plunger. The tied-up Rabbid dodged the blow. Kicking his feet, he managed to swing himself up onto the branch. He untied his ears, jumped down, grabbed a stick, and ran straight at the Rabbid with the toilet plunger.

"BWWWAAAAH!" he shouted as he ran.

WHAM! WHACK! THUMP! Soon the Rabbids were wildly fighting each other with sticks, plungers, and whatever else they could get their hands on.

Nearby, a teenager was lying under a tree, bored. "There's nothing to *do* in this stupid park," he said, looking at the paths and the tennis courts and the basketball courts and the pond with its paddleboats. Then he noticed the battling Rabbids.

"Aha!" he said. "Now *that* is hilarious!" His phone was in his hand (it was *always* in his hand, even when he was sleeping), so he held it up and started making a video of the Rabbid fight.

When the Rabbids took a short break, exhausted from running around and whacking each other, the teenager posted his video to the Internet. In no time at all, it was seen by millions of people all over the world.

Including Director Stern, the head of the Secret Government Agency for the Investigation of Intruders—Rabbid Division, also known as the SGAII-RD. Seeing the fighting Rabbids on the screen of his computer, Director Stern turned purple with anger.

"GLYKER!" he bellowed. "GET IN MY OFFICE! *NOW!!!*"

CHAPTER 2:

Glyker Goes Rabbid

In his crummy office at the SGAII-RD, Agent Glyker was leaning back in his chair, staring at the ceiling, dreaming of catching a Rabbid. When he heard his Uncle Jim (who was the head of the agency, and insisted on being called "Director Stern"), he fell backward onto the floor with a *CRASH!*

Agent Glyker scrambled to his feet, set his chair back up, and sprinted down the hallway to his

uncle's office. It was much bigger and nicer than Glyker's office. He peeked through the door.

"Yes, Uncle Ji— I mean, Director Stern?" he asked. "You wanted to see me?"

Director Stern scowled. "I don't *want* to see you, but I *have* to see you," he growled. "Look at this!" He spun his computer around so Glyker could see the screen.

A video showed three Rabbids whacking each other with sticks and toilet plungers. "Notice anything?" Director Stern hissed.

"Um, Rabbids really like toilet plungers?" Glyker guessed.

3,258,001 VIEWS

"THE VIEWS!" Stern shouted, pointing at the number displayed below the video. "OVER THREE MILLION VIEWS!"

Agent Glyker nodded. "Right," he said, not sure what Stern was getting at. "That's, um, a lot of views. I posted a video of this really cool bear at the zoo and it got, like, seven views. And I think six of them were me."

Stern slammed his hand down on the top of his desk. *WHAM!* "Too many views!" he said. "These Rabbid invaders have successfully infiltrated the Internet! It's part of their plan to take over planet Earth! THEY MUST BE STOPPED!"

Agent Glyker stood up straight and threw back his shoulders. "Yes, sir!" he barked. He was tempted to salute, but he knew from experience that his uncle didn't like that.

Director Stern paced around the room. "Somehow these invaders have become popular, and that's very bad. People don't realize how dangerous they are. One day the Rabbids are hitting each other to lull us into a false sense of security. The next day they're hitting *us*! And the *next* thing you know, they're RUNNING EVERYTHING!"

Glyker was nodding his head so vigorously he was starting to get a sore neck. Director Stern stopped pacing and shoved his face close to the agent's.

"And what are *you* doing to stop the Rabbids?" he snarled. "Sitting in your office and staring at the ceiling?"

Agent Glyker wondered if his uncle had installed a secret camera that let him see everything Glyker did in his office.

"As a matter of fact," Glyker said proudly, "I've been working on a new strategy to infiltrate the Rabbids' ranks. Would you like to see?"

Before Stern could answer, Glyker ran out of the office. When he returned a few moments later, he was wearing something quite surprising.

A Rabbid suit.

"I sewed it myself! Well, sewed and glued. Mostly glued, actually. Sewing is hard," Glyker explained with great enthusiasm. "It wasn't easy finding just the right material, but I think I nailed it!"

Director Stern stared at his nephew. He shook his head. "I'm not sure mysterious beings capable of taking over a planet are going to be fooled by a Halloween costume."

"Just count on me, sir!" Glyker promised,

saluting in spite of himself. "I've been practicing my Rabbid moves!"

He started moving around the office, doing a decent impression of a walking Rabbid. He even paused and wiggled his butt.

Director Stern sighed heavily. "Just go," he said.

CHAPTER 3:

What Is That Thing?

The three Rabbids were still in the big public park in the center of the city. They may not have gotten any piñata candy, but they were thoroughly enjoying themselves.

They'd found the park's large, beautiful fountain.

"Bwooooh," all three said when they first spotted the fountain spraying water high in the air. They ran down a grassy hill to reach the fountain as fast as their stubby legs could carry them.

After marching around the rim of the fountain, they started kicking and splashing water at each other. "BWAH HA HA HA!"

Now one of them was making his way toward the center of the fountain, planning to climb up to where the water spurted out. But before he could figure out the best way to reach the top, he heard one of his fellow Rabbids ask, "Bwah bwah BWAH?!"

Almost as if he were asking, "What is THAT?!"

The Rabbid climbing the fountain looked around to see what the other Rabbid was talking about. He saw the other two Rabbids pointing, so he looked in the direction they were indicating.

What he saw looked very strange.

From a small group of trees, a figure was walking across the grass toward them. It looked kind of like a Rabbid, but taller. Its eyes and mouth looked funny.

The strange figure raised its hand and said, "Bwah bwah!" Its voice sounded weird to the Rabbids.

"Bwuh?" the climbing Rabbid said, puzzled. He got down and joined the other two Rabbids. All three stared at the strange creature coming toward them.

They knew this was no Rabbid. But what was it?

When the creature had almost reached the fountain, the three Rabbids suddenly ran toward it. They circled around the weird figure, trying to figure out what it was.

The creature tried to get them to stop. It held up one hand and said, "Bwah!"

The Rabbids finally figured out what the thing was.

It was funny!

"BWAH HA HA HA HA HA HA!" they laughed,

pointing at the fake Rabbid. They laughed and laughed, rolling on the grass and laughing until they were exhausted.

This seemed to make the fake Rabbid mad. "Bwah bwah bwah bwah!" it said, trying to get them to stop laughing. It was shaking its fist at them.

One of the Rabbids noticed the toilet plunger he'd left in the grass while they were playing in the fountain. Suddenly he didn't feel tired any more. He picked up the plunger.

He ran over to the fake Rabbid and gave it a whack in the butt with the rubber end of the plunger. *WHAP!* Then he laughed again. "BWAH HA HA!"

The other two Rabbids thought this was a brilliant idea. They picked up their toilet plungers and ran at the fake Rabbid. It started running around the fountain, chased by the three real Rabbids waving their toilet plungers.

The three Rabbids soon caught up with the fake Rabbid. They surrounded it as it stood with his back to the fountain. They swung their plungers. It leaned back, dodging the plungers, and . . .

SPLOOSH!

The fake Rabbid fell right into the fountain! When it stood up, it was dripping wet. And its pretend fur was falling off!

"Bwah?" asked the Rabbids, puzzled. Why was the weird creature falling apart?

The fake Rabbid tried to pull itself back together, but the more it tried, the more it came apart. Finally it climbed out of the fountain and ran back into the trees, slipping in the grass a couple of times.

The three Rabbids watched it go. Then they broke into loud laughter again. "BWAH HA HA HA HA HA HA!!!"

CHAPTER 4:
Back to the Drawing Board

Agent Glyker squished into his small apartment and closed the door behind him. His plan had utterly failed. He was sore from being whacked with toilet plungers. He was sopping wet. And his Rabbid disguise had fallen apart the minute it touched the water. (Probably because he'd glued it together instead of sewing it. But sewing was hard.)

Still, was Agent Glyker discouraged? Dismayed? Ready to give up?

No! He was not!

"I just have to come up with a better plan," he said to himself. When he was alone in his dingy little apartment, he often talked to himself. It helped him think.

He paced around his tiny living room, thinking.

The Rabbid disguise had seemed like the perfect way to get close enough to the Rabbids to grab one of them. But getting that close had turned out to be dangerous. He had the bruises to prove it.

"How can I get close enough to the Rabbids to gather lots of good intel about them without putting myself in danger?" Danger wasn't the part of being a spy that Agent Glyker liked. He liked the secret stuff. The hidden stuff. The high-tech gadgets . . .

High-tech! That was the answer!

"A remote-controlled robot Rabbid!" he shouted. What a great idea! Glyker could build a robot that looked like a Rabbid. Then he could control it from a safe distance, so he wouldn't be

29

in any danger of getting hurt. Perfect!

After putting on dry clothes, Agent Glyker hurried out to buy everything he'd need to build a robot Rabbid. He'd finish it right away, even if he had to stay up all night working on it.

And that's exactly what happened.

He was so excited to get started that

he began building it right there in his car.

As the sun was coming up the next morning, Agent Glyker put the finishing touches on his robot Rabbid. He picked up the remote control and pushed the button to make the robot walk forward. *Whirrr...*

It worked!

But would the Rabbids think it was real?

CHAPTER 5:

Robot Rabbid

The three Rabbids ran through the city, looking for something interesting.

They found something *very* interesting.

A cement truck finished pouring fresh cement for a new sidewalk. Workers smoothed over the wet cement. Then they put stakes in the ground beside the sidewalk, tied strings to the stakes to keep people out, and left to go pour another sidewalk in another part of the city.

The Rabbids watched the slowly spinning cement truck drive away. They ran over to the fresh new sidewalk with its wet gray cement.

One of the Rabbids considered himself the leader of this little group. (It wasn't at all clear that the other two Rabbids agreed with him.) He pushed the other Rabbids back and pointed to his chest. "Bwah bwah bwah bwah!" he said, seeming to mean that he would go first.

He carefully stuck his foot into the wet cement, then pulled it out. *Shhhwomp!* An impression of his foot stayed in the cement! He was delighted!

When the other two Rabbids saw what he'd done, they eagerly stepped over the strings and put their feet in the cement. *Shhhwomp! Shhhwomp!* They pointed at the indentations in the cement and laughed. "BWAH HA HA!"

Then they did their hands. And their faces. And their butts. Soon they were lying in the wet cement making cement angels!

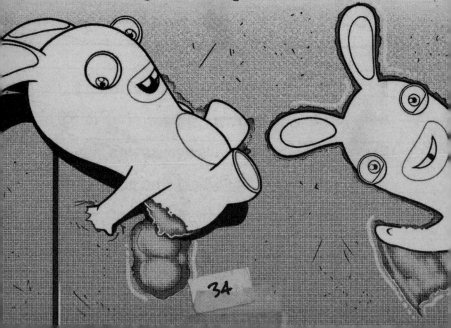

But the cement was drying quickly. When they tried to get up from their cement angels, they found it wasn't that easy. The cement was starting to stick. With a mighty effort, one Rabbid managed to heave himself up out of the cement. *Shhhhhhwoompf!*

He helped pull the next Rabbid out, and then together the two of them yanked out the third Rabbid, who was *really* starting to stick in the cement!

Their backs were covered with cement. Luckily, they jumped in a nearby fountain (which they would have jumped in anyway) and the cement came off. Then they went back to the ruined sidewalk to admire what they'd done. Footprints! Handprints! Face prints! Butt prints! It was beautiful! They kept saying "Bwooh!" and "Bwaah!" over and over, thrilled with their artwork.

Then they heard a strange sound behind them. *Whirrr . . .*

The three Rabbids whipped around and saw . . . a Rabbid! Coming straight toward them! Its walk was a little peculiar— it swayed from side to side a bit—but it definitely looked like a Rabbid.

The Rabbid who considered himself the leader stepped forward and held up one hand. "Bwah bwah

bwah bwah bwah!" he said, greeting the newcomer.

Slowly, the unknown Rabbid lifted its hand.

The leader Rabbid squinted at the stranger, thinking. Could he trust this Rabbid?

Suddenly, behind them there was a low growl. *Rrrrrr!* The Rabbids turned around and saw a big, fierce dog!

The new Rabbid didn't hesitate. It lifted both its arms and headed straight toward the menacing dog.

The dog didn't know what to make of this fearless creature. It tucked its tail, whimpered, turned around, and ran.

"BWAH HA HA HA HA!" laughed the Rabbids. They clapped the new

Rabbid on the back, congratulating it on a job well done.

And when they started to walk away, the three Rabbids turned back and beckoned with their arms, inviting the new Rabbid to come with them.

From his hiding place behind a nearby bench, Agent Glyker grinned. Success at last!

Then he yawned. He hadn't gotten any sleep the night before. It wouldn't hurt to go home and catch up on his sleep. The robot would be gathering fantastic intel with its built-in video camera. Later, he could electronically track the robot and find out exactly where the Rabbids were. Simple!

Glyker set the robot on automatic pilot and headed back to his apartment, yawning again.

That was another great thing about robots. They never needed to sleep.

CHAPTER 6:
Nighttime Rabbids

The sun had set and the city was dark. But the Rabbids were still running through the streets, showing their new friend the sights.

As they ran down a dark alley, they saw light spilling out through an open door. The leader peered in and was amazed by what he saw.

A large man dressed in white pants, a white shirt, a white apron, and a white cap was making noodles. The Rabbids had stumbled upon an Italian restaurant where a cook worked through the night making fresh pasta for the next day's customers.

The cook hung a fresh batch of noodles up to dry. Then he went into the next room for a short break.

The leader walked right into the kitchen, followed by his two fellow Rabbids and the robot Rabbid.

The Rabbids climbed up onto the table to investigate. Since the table was covered with flour, they soon were too.

"Bwoooh," said the leader, pulling a long noodle off the drying rack. He whipped it around in the air, then threw it right at the robot!

Fwap! The robot just stood there with the noodle stuck to its head. It didn't seem to mind at all.

"BWAH HA HA HA!" laughed the three Rabbids. In no time at all, noodles were flying through the air, hitting all the Rabbids and sticking to their bodies!

Inspired by the robot, one of the Rabbids took a big handful of noodles and plopped it on top of his own head. Using the side of a big metal pot as a mirror, he arranged the noodles into a lovely hairdo. (Well, *he* thought it was lovely.)

The cook returned from his break. "HEY! WHAT ARE YOU DOING IN HERE?!" he yelled. He grabbed a wooden spoon and started chasing the Rabbids around the kitchen, shooing them out of his work space.

"BWAH HA HA!" the Rabbids laughed. They grabbed more noodles as they ran, plopping them on their heads. The cook kept swinging his spoon at them, but he missed every time. The Rabbids and the robot were too quick for him.

They scooted out the door and into the night. "AND DON'T COME BACK!" the cook yelled after them.

Agent Glyker was lying in his bed, having kicked off the covers. He awoke from a dream where the president had given him a medal for stopping the Rabbid invasion. *I'll sleep just a little while longer,* he thought. *Maybe I'll dream that same dream again. That was so nice. . . .*

Within seconds he was snoring.

The Rabbids found a lovely place to sleep: a big garbage container with a lid. They climbed in, rustling around in the trash before they went to sleep. The three of them found old clothes and pieces of discarded aluminum foil to wear, just for the fun of it.

As they settled down to sleep, they noticed the robot wasn't with them. They lifted the lid of the trash container and looked out.

There was the robot, just standing there.

47

"Bwah bwah bwah bwah bwah!" they called, inviting the robot to join them in the trash container.

But it just stood there.

With a *suit yourself* shrug, the Rabbids closed the lid and settled back down in the trash to sleep. But just as they were nodding off, they heard . . .

Boop! Beep! Buzz! Whirr! Beep!

They sat up, annoyed by the noises. When they opened the lid again, they saw that the robot was making the sounds. They yelled at it to shut up:

"Bwah bwah bwah bwah bwah!"

Boop! Beep! Buzz! Whirr! Beep!

One of the Rabbids climbed out of the trash container and stood right in front of the robot. "Bwah . . . bwah . . . BWAH!" he said slowly.

Boop! Beep! Buzz! Whirr! Beep!

Frustrated, he whacked the robot. Without knowing it, he pressed a hidden button that put the robot into a sleep mode. It slumped a little, and got quiet. It was still standing, but at least it wasn't beeping and booping.

"Bwah," the Rabbid said with a satisfied nod. He climbed back into the trash container and soon fell asleep.

CHAPTER 7:

Heavy Metal Rabbids

Early the next morning the three Rabbids woke up, stretched, and climbed out of the big trash container. They still had noodles on their heads. And they were still wearing the odd bits of junk and clothing they'd found in the container.

The robot was just standing there, a little slumped.

One of the Rabbids raised his hand and greeted the robot. "Bwah bwah bwah!"

The robot said nothing.

The Rabbid tried again. "Bwah bwah bwah!"

Still nothing.

Annoyed, the Rabbid gave the robot a whack. Without knowing it, he hit the robot's wake-up button. *Boop! Beep! Buzz! Whirr! Beep!*

The Rabbids remembered these noises. They were the same ones that had kept them awake the night before.

They decided maybe they'd had enough of this weird Rabbid who didn't talk and made such annoying sounds. They'd thought maybe it'd be fun to have around, but it wasn't.

They whispered among themselves ("bwah bwah bwah bwah") and then strolled away from the robot, whistling.

The robot followed them.

The Rabbids looked back and saw the weird Rabbid following them. They started walking faster.

The robot moved faster too.

The Rabbids started to run! But the robot kept up with them. *Whirr! Beep! Boop!*

The leader screeched to a halt. He whirled around and got in the robot's face. "BWAH BWAH BWOH BWOOH BWEE BWAH!" he yelled.

But when he turned around and started to leave, the robot still followed him and the other two Rabbids.

Eventually the three Rabbids got so annoyed with the robot that they started screaming at it in the scariest voices they could make. They growled! They screeched! They howled! They barked! They *screamed*! "BWAAAAAAH!"

Nearby, a group of teenagers was hanging out in a small park. "Whoah!"

one of them said. "What is that?!"

They listened to the crazy sounds the Rabbids were making for another minute or two. Then one of them said, "I think I know what that is. Come on!"

He got up to investigate. His friends followed him. They found the Rabbids, dressed in scraps of trash, sporting long noodle hair, screaming at the robot. The teenager smiled.

"Awesome," he said. "This must be one of the heavy metal bands in town for the big concert at the amphitheater!"

Immediately he held up his phone to make a video.

When they saw what he was doing, his friends held up their phones too. One of them asked, "How do they do that with their voices? I mean, without totally wrecking their throats?"

Another guy just shook his head. "Who knows, dude? They're professionals."

The first teenager smiled again. Two smiles in one day

was very unusual for him. (He preferred frowning.) "This is going to get, like, a zillion views," he said. When the Rabbids paused for a moment, he posted his video to the Internet.

He was right. The video of "Heavy Metal Rabbids" went viral instantly. Friends sent it to friends, until millions of people all over the world had seen it. And liked it.

Unfortunately for Agent Glyker, one of those millions of viewers was Director Stern. But he didn't like it at all. . . .

CHAPTER 8:

To the Amphitheater

Bing bing bongy bong bong! Bing bing bongy bong bong! Agent Glyker slowly woke up, feeling groggy after so many hours of sleep. What was that sound he was hearing? It was familiar . . .

"Oh! My phone!" he said, reaching for his cell phone. The screen told him that Uncle Jim was calling him. He braced himself and touched the screen. "Good morning, Director Stern—"

"GLYKER! WHAT IN THE NAME OF THE RABBIDS ARE YOU DOING?!" Stern bellowed. "THE INTERNET'S BEING COMPLETELY TAKEN OVER BY RABBIDS AND WHERE ARE YOU? LYING IN BED?"

Glyker wondered if Stern had installed cameras in his bedroom. He jumped up and started yanking on a pair of pants, right over his pajamas. "No, sir! I've got the Rabbids under robotic surveillance! I'm going to check on them right now!"

"Well, you'd better hurry!" Stern growled.

"There are several new videos of the Rabbids wearing these weird outfits and screaming at each other. The Rabbids are getting MORE popular, not less! What do I pay you for, anyway?"

"Don't worry, sir," Glyker said reassuringly as he put his right foot into the left leg of his pants. "I've got everything under control."

Glyker ended the call and switched to the app that showed him where his robot was. "I sure hope my robot's still with those Rabbids," he muttered as he headed out the door of his apartment.

The Rabbids had gotten tired of yelling at the robot. Nothing they said, screamed, or growled seemed to have any effect on it anyway.

The oldest teenager walked up to the Rabbids. They turned and stared at him.

"You guys sound awesome," he said. "Can't wait to hear you at the concert."

They kept staring, having no idea what he was talking about.

"Need a ride to the amphitheater?" the teenager asked.

The Rabbids turned to each other and shrugged. "Bwuh?" they asked.

"Oh, I get it," the dude said. "Before you agree to a ride, you wanna check out my car. Understood."

He ran off. The Rabbids waited, wondering what was going to happen.

The teenager pulled up in his car. It was black, with a big skull painted on the hood and flames on the sides. The wheels had huge spinning silver rims.

"Bwoooooooh!" said all three Rabbids.

Boop! Beep! Whirr! said the robot.

The dude rolled down his window and beckoned with his arm. "Hop in!" The Rabbids ran to jump into the car, and the robot followed. As the car peeled out, the Rabbids hung out the windows, grinning and yelling, "BWAAAH!"

Soon they arrived at the city's amphitheater, a huge arena that could hold thousands of fans. All day different heavy metal bands were performing. Hundreds of fans were wandering around outside, waiting for their favorite bands to play.

As the Rabbids climbed down out of the car, several people noticed them and pointed. "Look!" one guy said. "It's those little dudes from the videos! They're awesome!"

Fans crowded around the Rabbids, taking pictures and videos with their phones. The Rabbids enjoyed the attention, and the robot followed the

Rabbids.

The teenager who had driven the Rabbids to the amphitheater said, "Let 'em through! Let the band through!"

When the security guys saw all the attention the Rabbids were getting, they let them go right into the amphitheater and onto the stage. When they stepped onto the stage, everyone cheered!

The Rabbids stood there, not sure what to do.

The fans waited. And waited. And waited.

The Rabbids stood onstage, looking around the huge amphitheater.

Finally one of the heavy metal fans grew impatient. "Come on!" he shouted. "Play something!" He threw an empty soda can and hit the leader Rabbid right in the head. *Bonk!*

"BWAAAAH!" he screamed, more angry than hurt. The crowd roared! They loved it!

Another one of the Rabbids tried a loud growling yell to see what would happen. "BWOOOOH!" The crowd loved that, too!

All three Rabbids started screaming, howling, growling, and roaring. The crowd went wild, pounding their feet on the floor of the arena. One of the heavy metal bands (a new, unpopular band that was still waiting for its big break) got an idea. They started playing, accompanying the Rabbids' screams with loud, ear-piercing drums and guitars. The crowd went even crazier!

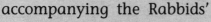

Even the robot chimed in. *Boop! Beep! Whirr!*

Outside, Agent Glyker pulled up in his beat-up old car. He was surprised that the robot's monitoring app had led him to the city's biggest amphitheater.

He was even more surprised when he got inside.

71

CHAPTER 9:

A Crazy Concert

Agent Glyker immediately saw that the Rabbids and his robot were onstage! The Rabbids were snarling and growling, pretending to play toilet plungers and mops as if they were guitars. They had noodles on their heads, and they were wearing weird scraps of clothing and aluminum foil.

"BWAH BWOH BWEE BWEE BWAAAAARRR!!!"

The people in the audience were moving in time with the music. Some were even saying "Bwah!"

and "Bwor!" along with the Rabbids. And almost everyone in the amphitheater was recording the Rabbids on their phones. More videos to go viral! The Rabbids would be more popular than ever, and Director Stern would be absolutely furious! So furious that Glyker would probably get fired.

I've got to get them off that stage, Glyker thought.

He quickly made his way down the aisle to the edge of the stage, but when he tried to climb up, he was stopped by two big security guards.

"WHERE DO YOU THINK YOU'RE GOING?" they yelled. They had to yell to be heard over the music.

Glyker pulled out his SGAII-RD badge and showed it to the guards. "I'm a secret agent! I'm here to stop those Rabbid intruders!"

"WHAT?" yelled one of the guards.

"I THINK HE SAID HE'S AN ANT WHO WANTS TO MOP THE RABID COMPUTERS!" the other guard shouted back.

The guards refused to let Glyker onto the stage. He wrote down Stern's phone number on a piece of paper and pointed to it. "Call my boss! He'll vouch for me!" One of the guards finally shrugged, pulled out his cell phone, and started dialing. He walked away, looking for a place where he could hear.

While he waited, Glyker watched desperately as the Rabbids ran around the stage, yelling and howling. Then he spotted his robot, standing onstage beeping and booping.

"My robot! Of course!" he said, pulling out his remote control. He started working the buttons, and the robot started moving toward the group of Rabbids. "If my robot can just grab one of the Rabbids . . ."

Inspired by the fast, loud music, the Rabbids had started running toward each other at full speed and slamming into each other. The crowd loved this, applauding and cheering.

So when one of the Rabbids saw the robot coming toward him, he ran at it as fast as he could, leaped into the air, and slammed into it! *WHAM!* The robot went flying off the stage and landed at Glyker's feet.

79

"My robot!" Glyker said, kneeling down to see if the robot was broken.

Just then the big security guard came back. "Oh, so now you've got a robot?" he asked skeptically.

"What did my boss say?" Glyker asked. "Did he tell you it was okay for me to go onstage and get the Rabbids?"

The guard shook his head. "He refused to talk to me. The minute he heard the music in the background, he said he hated that kind of noise and hung up."

Glyker lost it. "I can't believe it! That idiot! Uncle Jim can be such a stupid, stubborn, maddening, obnoxious—"

But Glyker's angry rant was interrupted when he noticed what was happening on the stage. Despite the best efforts of the security guards, audience members were climbing up onstage and destroying everything in a frenzy. The Rabbids had started it, deciding it would be fun to run right into the drums and slam guitars into the speakers.

Glyker tried to make his way to one of the Rabbids, but before he could reach them, he saw one of them pull a remote control out and push a button.

"NO!" he yelled, knowing from experience what was coming next.

FWOOSH! The big doors behind the stage blew open, and a yellow-and-blue spaceship flew in! It looked like a flying submarine with a Rabbid's face on the front.

If the crowd had been going crazy before, now they went absolutely bonkers! They loved the spaceship! They all rushed onstage, so there was no way Glyker could get through the mob to reach the Rabbids.

The three Rabbids ran into the spaceship. Before its door closed, the Rabbids took a deep bow. The crowd roared! *FWOOOM!* The spaceship took off and flew out of the amphitheater, disappearing into the sky.

Glyker stood in Director Stern's office with his robot while his uncle chewed him out. "So you didn't catch a SINGLE Rabbid! And now there are HUNDREDS of videos of them on the Internet! Getting MILLIONS of views!"

"Um, yes," Glyker said, shifting his feet nervously. "But my robot did gather a lot of intel!

Just let me play back what it recorded while it was

with the Rabbids. . . ."

Agent Glyker fumbled nervously with the robot's controls. Suddenly the robot projected a video onto the wall. In it, Glyker was talking to the security guard at the amphitheater: "That idiot! Uncle Jim can be such a stupid, stubborn, maddening, obnoxious—"

Glyker managed to shut it off. But it was too late. Stern was turning purple with rage. He managed to speak without yelling, biting each word off one at a time. "Why . . . shouldn't . . . I . . . fire . . . you . . . right . . . now?"

Glyker thought hard. He hated to play this card, but it was the only one he could think of. "Because my mom would be mad at you? I mean, you are her little brother, so you really should be nice to her baby boy. . . ."

Director Stern glared at his nephew for a full minute. Then he blew air out through his nose. "Just get out of my office. AND TAKE THIS STUPID ROBOT WITH YOU!"

89

Glyker's To-Do List:

1. File expense report to be reimbursed for robot parts.

2. Download heavy metal albums and study lyrics for clues about Rabbid motives.

3. Find out what kind of cake Uncle Jim likes best.

4. Ask Mom to bake a cake for Uncle Jim.

5. Find out who infiltrated my online dating profile and replaced my personal photo with a picture of a toilet.

large mouth

bent tongue